Cinderella

and me!

For Samuel, Martha and Lilly – E.B.

First published 2015 by Nosy Crow Ltd
The Crow's Nest, 10a Lant Street
London SE1 1QR
www.nosycrow.com
ISBN 978 0 85763 470 2 (HB)
ISBN 978 0 85763 471 9 (PB)
Nosy Crow and associated logos are trademarks
and/or registered trademarks of Nosy Crow Ltd
Text © Nosy Crow 2015
Illustrations © Nosy Crow 2011
The right of Ed Bryan to be identified as the
illustrator of this work has been asserted.

A CIP catalogue record for this book is available from the British Library.
Printed in China
Papers used by Nosy Crow are made from wood grown in
sustainable forests.
1 3 5 7 9 8 6 4 2 (HB)
1 3 5 7 9 8 6 4 2 (PB)

Cinderella

Nosy Crow

Illustrated by
Ed Bryan

Once upon a time, there was a kind
and lovely girl called **Cinderella**.

Cinderella had to clean the house all day long.
She had no nice clothes and was covered in dust
and dirt from working in the kitchen.

But worst of all, poor Cinderella lived with her stepmother and two **mean** stepsisters.

Cinderella lived in a country ruled by a **king**, and that king had a **son** who was a good and gentle prince.

"It's time you got married," said the king. "I'll give a **grand ball** so you can meet all the young ladies in the land."

And the next day, an invitation arrived at Cinderella's house.

--To the ladies of the house--
the King invites you to a

Royal Ball

with dancing and ice cream
at The Palace.
°o°
Please wear your very finest ballgown.

Cinderella's stepmother and stepsisters were all very **excited**. "The prince is **sure** to fall in love with **one** of you!" said the stepmother. "How wonderful!"

They made **SO** much **noise** that Cinderella came in from the kitchen. "May **I** go to the ball?" she asked.

"Don't be silly, Cinderella. The prince would **never** marry **you!**" said her stepmother.

On the night of the ball, Cinderella had to help her stepsisters get ready.

"Fetch my **tiara!**" shrieked one stepsister.

"Find my **hair ribbon!**" shouted the other.

After everyone had left to go to the palace, Cinderella cried and cried because she really wanted to go to the ball herself.

As Cinderella sobbed by the fire, a friendly-looking lady **suddenly** appeared.

"I am your fairy godmother," she said.
"I am here to make your dream come **true**.
Come into the garden with me!"

Out in the moonlit garden, the fairy godmother quickly got to work. "We need three **mice** and a **pumpkin**, Cinderella! Please bring them to me."

With a wave of her wand, the fairy godmother turned the pumpkin into a beautiful **carriage**, two mice became prancing **horses**, and the third mouse became a **coachman**.

Cinderella's ragged clothes
became a beautiful **ballgown**
and glass **slippers** appeared
on her dusty feet.

Cinderella was very happy, but her fairy godmother had a warning for her. "The magic only lasts until midnight," she said. "You **must** be home by then!"

Cinderella rode to the palace in
her magnificent carriage.

As Cinderella entered the ballroom, **everyone** turned to look at her. "She looks familiar," said the stepsisters. "I'm **sure** we've seen her somewhere before."

Straight away, the prince asked Cinderella to dance.

Cinderella and the prince danced **all** night long.

But Cinderella had forgotten her fairy godmother's warning. Suddenly, the clock struck midnight.

"Oh no," cried Cinderella. "I must go!"

DING!

DONG!

As Cinderella ran from the ballroom,
one of her glass slippers **fell off.**

The prince picked it up.
"I will marry the girl whose foot fits
this shoe," he said.

Moments later, Cinderella's carriage turned back into a **pumpkin** and the horses and coachman became **mice** again. Cinderella found herself wearing her **ragged clothes** once more.

The prince **searched** for Cinderella for weeks and months.

At last, he arrived at Cinderella's house. Her stepsisters tried to **push** their feet into the glass slipper, but it did **not** fit.

Then **Cinderella** looked in from the kitchen. "Would you please bring the shoe over here so I can try it on?" she said.

Cinderella's foot slipped easily into the slipper.

"It's a **perfect** fit," she said.
"**I knew** I'd find you in the end!" cried the prince.

The prince and Cinderella had a **wonderful** wedding. Even Cinderella's stepmother and stepsisters were invited.

And Cinderella and the prince lived
happily ever after.